# DANNY'S IN THE D̶O̶G̶H̶O̶U̶S̶E

© 2017 Kathy Joseph and Brett Thompson/GLC Alpaca Place
All rights reserved. Printed in the United States.
No part of this book may be reproduced or copied in any form
without the written permission of the copyright owners.

Written by Kathy Joseph
Illustrated by Brett Thompson
Editorial development by friends and family
Visit us at www.glcalpacaplace

ISBN-13: 978-1546946205 International
ISBN-10: 1546946209i National

THIS BOOK BELONGS TO_____

Look for these words in the story:

alpaca
alpacas spit
cria
cush
hum or hmmm
neck wrestling
pronking

You can find them in the Glossary
in the back of the book.

# CAST OF CHARACTERS

Belanca, Mamma Alpaca 1

Bim Bim, Mama Alpaca 2

Cory

Danny

Eden

Grayson

Hannah

Petie

Splash

"Good morning my baby cria," said the mama alpaca to her baby alpaca. "Did you have a good night's rest?"

"Yes Mama," hummed Petie. "I had the perfect place to cush last night, right next to you."

1

"Come, have some breakfast and then go out to the pasture and play with the other crias. It is important that young alpacas get plenty of exercise to make their legs grow strong."

After breakfast Petie looked
at the gate that led to the
pasture and saw
Danny in the doorway.

"But Mama, I can't get out,"
hummed Petie.
"Danny's in the doorway."

3

Mama looked, and sure enough there was Danny in the doorway.
"Well, you might have to ask him if he would let you out.
Hmmm, or you could just go around him," Mama replied.

"But Mama, you know that alpacas are not rude. You taught me to wait and not barge through, and I don't think there is enough room for me to get through without bumping into him."

"You are right," said Mama. "I guess you have a little problem to solve, or you can simply wait until Danny's not in the doorway."

4

So the crias thought about it and decided that they would just play inside the corral and wait for Danny to leave the doorway. They started romping around the corral, but because there wasn't a lot of room, the crias accidently bumped into some of the mama alpacas.

5

"Please be careful," said one of the mama alpacas. "Why don't you crias go out into the pasture to play?"

"We can't," replied Splash. "Danny's in the doorway."

"Hmmm," said the second mama. "You need to figure out a way to get into the pasture to play or cush quietly in the corner of the corral so that no one gets hurt."

7

The young crias looked at each other and decided that it was too nice a day just to cush quietly. So they began working on a plan to get to the pasture.

"Maybe we could go under him," said Petie.

But just as Petie tried to crawl under, Danny moved one of his hind legs forward so Petie couldn't get through.

A little discouraged, Petie went back to the other crias.

"I guess we are just going to have to play more carefully until Danny's not in the doorway," hummed Cory.

"That won't be any fun," said Petie. "I'll neck wrestle you, and the loser will have to go ask Danny to move out of the doorway."

"You are on," said Cory.

11

The boys wrestled while the other crias cheered them on.
Finally, realizing that no one was going to win,
they called it a tie. "Well," said Splash, "now what are we going to do?"

Pretty soon all of the crias were lined up impatiently staring at Danny, waiting for him to get out of the doorway.

13

Strangely enough, even the constant stares from the crias were not enough to move Danny from the doorway where he continued to stand.

"I know," said Grayson, "let's pretend that we were just given some fresh hay."

"Yeah, and he will get out of the doorway," Splash hummed in.

"Exactly! Then we can go out to the pasture to play," Cory added.

So all the crias pretended to munch on some hay.

Humming loudly so that Danny would hear them from the doorway, the crias were saying,

"Yeah, we never get fresh hay first thing in the morning."

"Hmmmm, this is so good."

"This is the best ever."

The crias continued to pretend to eat while glancing over their shoulders to see if Danny was interested in joining them. But to their disappointment, Danny was still in the doorway.

15

"OK," said Splash, "That's it.
I'm just going to jump over him.
I'll get a running start and
simply fly over the top."
He could picture this perfectly
in his mind. So when he was
ready, he summoned enough
courage and began running
full speed. Faster. Faster.
Faster.

But just as he was
ready to leap into the air,
Splash slammed on his brakes
and came to a screeching halt just
before crashing into Danny.

16

Hanging his head in shame, he returned to the herd of crias.

"What happened?" asked Grayson.

"I chickened out," replied Splash. "The closer I got to Danny, the bigger he looked. I was afraid that I couldn't do it. I knew if I crashed into him, he would spit on me."

"That's Okay," encouraged Cory. "At least you tried."

"This is ridiculous," cried Petie. "I can't believe that we are still stuck in this corral on a beautiful day like this. I wish we could just get out to the pasture."

"But how?" questioned Eden. "We have tried to go under him, around him, over him and even trick him. But after all of that, Danny's still in the doorway."

"Well there is only one thing left to do," said little Hannah, "and I am going to do it!"

All of the crias were in awe as little Hannah marched right up to Danny, who was still in the doorway. They could see her talking to him when all of a sudden

20

Danny stepped out of the doorway
and into the pasture.

21

Immediately all of
the crias cheered!

22

They ran through the doorway into the pasture.

After pronking twice around the pasture in sheer joy,

24

the crias came up to Hannah. "How did you do that?" Eden asked.

"You are our hero!" Splash hummed loudly.

25

"What did you say to him to get him out of the doorway?" asked Grayson.

26

"It was very easy," blushed Hannah, "I simply asked him if he would please move out of the doorway so we could play in the pasture."

"That was it?" They all cried.

"That was it," replied Hannah. "Oh, and Danny added, 'I'd be happy to. All you needed to do was ask. But I did enjoy all of the silly attempts to get me to move.'"

27

"I guess I learned something," mumbled Petie.

"What's that?" questioned Hannah.

"The first thing you should do when you want something is simply ask," replied Petie.

"Hmmmmmmmm," everyone hummed in.

28

# Alpaca Glossary

## alpaca

These gentle animals came to the U.S. from South America. They are cousins to llamas and camels and are raised for their fabulous wool.

## alpacas spit

They spit to show displeasure, stress, or if they feel threatened.

## cria

This is what we call a baby or young alpaca.

## cush

This is the resting postition of alpacas when they lie down with all four legs underneath them. Their heads and necks are in an upright position.

## neck wrestling

Crias neck wrestle in a playful way to learn how to wrestle when they become adults. Adult alpacas neck wrestle to establish their position in the herd.

## pronking

Alpacas leap in the air with an arched back and stiff legs. They usually do this when they are happy or playing.

# Cast of Characters

Belanca, Mama Alpaca 1

Danny

Hannah

Bim Bim, Mama Alpaca 2

Eden

Petie

Cory

Grayson

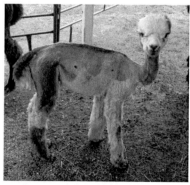
Splash

About the Author
Kathy Joseph is a retired band director who fell in love with alpacas and began raising
them for her future retirement hobby. She lives in Grand Junction, Colorado,
with her alpaca family. Spending the past 15 years with these amazing
animals has brought great joy into her life. In the spring of 2017 she saw Danny standing
in the doorway of the corral while other alpacas waited to get to the pasture. This
triggered the idea of "Danny's in the Doorway."

About the Illustrator
Brett Thompson has been drawing and painting since he was just a little boy. He has lived in
Rifle, Colorado; NYC; Tokyo, Japan; Las Cruces, NM and currently resides in Grand Junction, Colorado,
drawing characters in all the various places he has lived.

52042220R10022

Made in the USA
San Bernardino, CA
09 August 2017